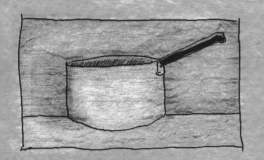

狐狸首先提出，他邀请鹤来吃晚餐…
当鹤抵达狐狸的家时，她看到柜上放置着各式各样不同颜色的盘子，
大的、高的、矮的、小的。
桌上放着两只平底浅碟。

鹤用她那长而薄的鸟嘴往碟上啄食，但不论她怎样尝试，
也无法喝到一口汤。

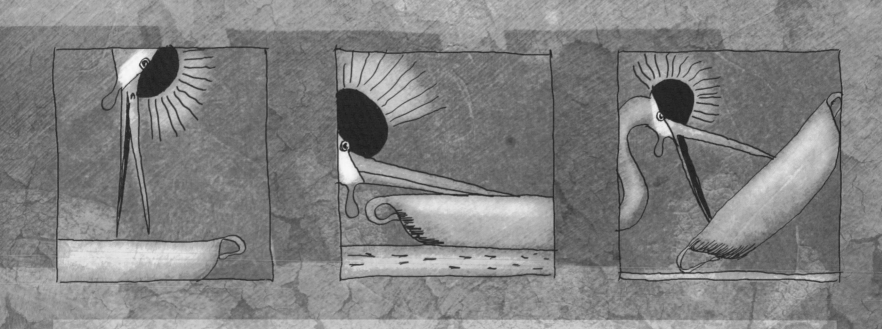

Crane pecked and she picked with her long thin beak. But no matter
how hard she tried she could not get even a sip of the soup.

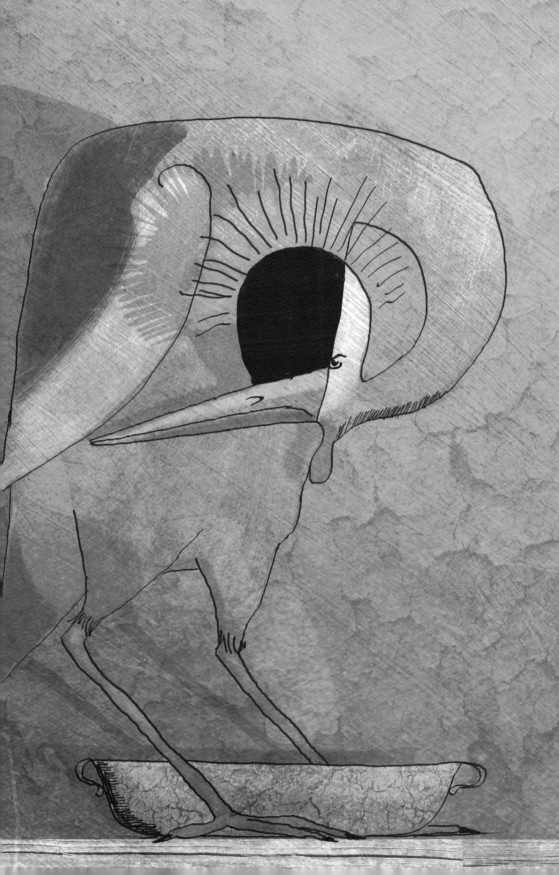

狐狸一面望着鹤吃力一面窃笑，
他把他的汤送到唇边，呷咂、啜吸、
咕嘟的将汤都喝干。
「嗳呀！真美味！」他嘲笑说，
并用他的爪背拭抹他的胡子，
「啊，鹤呀，你还未动过你的汤，」
狐狸假笑着说，「真不好意思，
你不喜欢这汤，」他说道，
并尽量避免轻蔑地笑。

Fox watched Crane struggling and sniggered.
He lifted his own soup to his lips, and with
a SIP, SLOP, SLURP he lapped it all up.
"Ahhhh, delicious!" he scoffed, wiping his
whiskers with the back of his paw.
"Oh Crane, you haven't touched your soup,"
said Fox with a smirk. "I AM sorry you
didn't like it," he added, trying not to snort
with laughter.

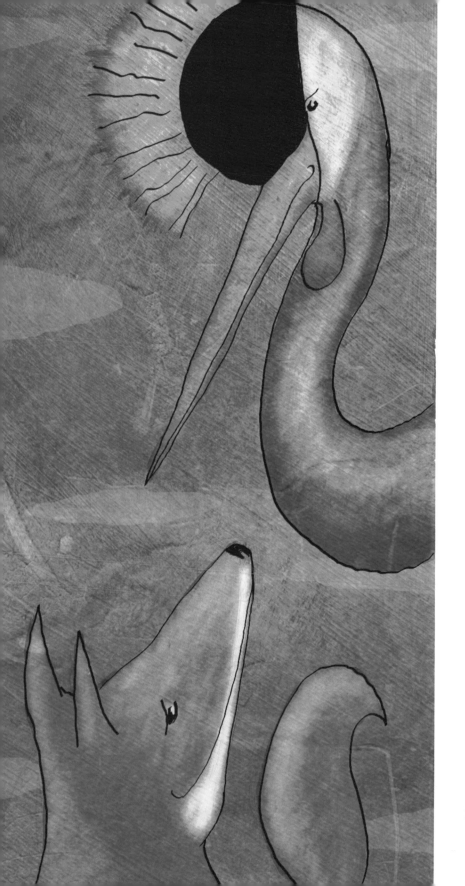

鹤默不作声，她看看晚餐，又看看碟子，
然后微笑地望着狐狸。
「亲爱的狐狸，多谢你的好意，」鹤有礼貌
地说，「请让我回敬你 –
来我的家吃饭吧。」

当狐狸到达时，窗门大开，一股香味溢出，
狐狸抬高他的鼻子去闻，他的嘴巴垂涎，
肚子隆隆作响，他舔舐他的嘴唇。

Crane said nothing. She looked at the meal. She looked
at the dish. She looked at Fox, and smiled.
"Dear Fox, thank you for your kindness," said Crane
politely. "Please let me repay you – come to dinner at
my house."

When Fox arrived the window was open. A delicious
smell drifted out. Fox lifted his snout and sniffed. His
mouth watered. His stomach rumbled. He licked his lips.

「亲爱的狐狸，请进来，」鹤说着，
优雅地展开她的翅膀。
狐狸冲过她，看到柜上放置着
各式各样不同颜色的盘子，红色的、
蓝色的、旧的、新的。
桌上放着两只盘子，
两只高窄的盘子。

"My dear Fox, do come in," said Crane,
extending her wing graciously.
Fox pushed past. He saw dishes of
every colour and kind lined the shelves.
Red ones, blue ones, old ones, new ones.
The table was set with two dishes.
Two tall narrow dishes.

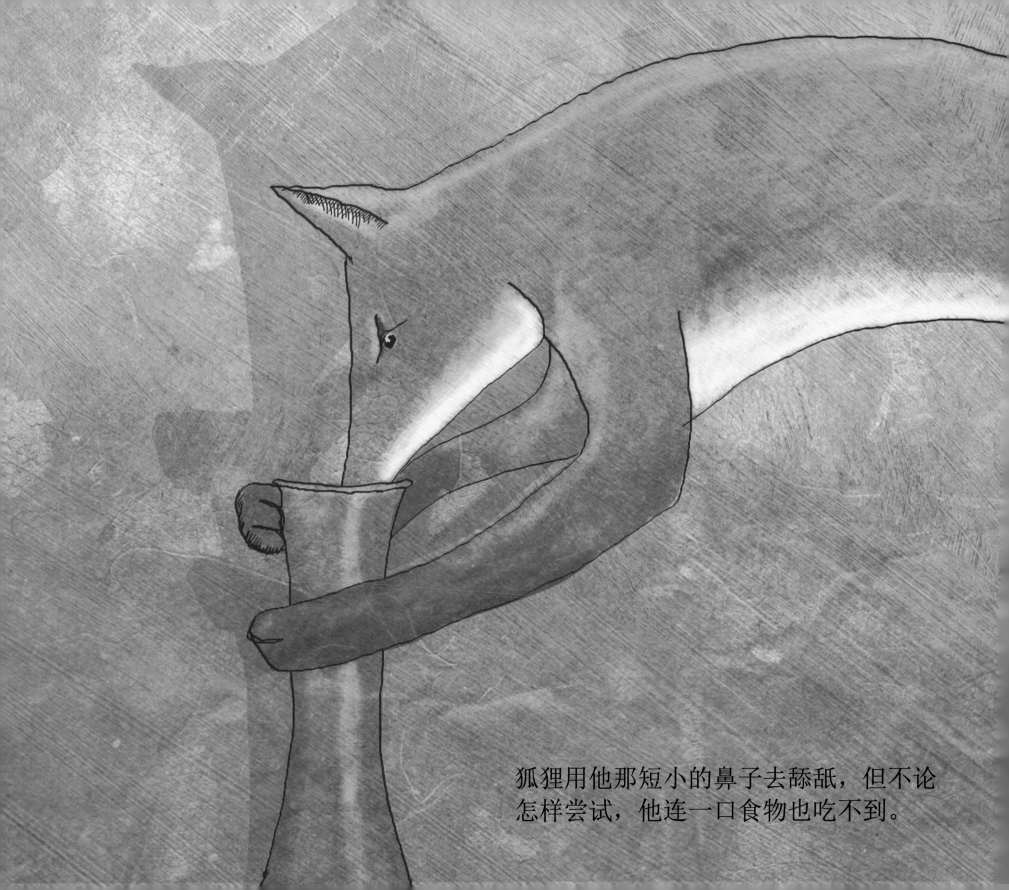

狐狸用他那短小的鼻子去舔舐，但不论怎样尝试，他连一口食物也吃不到。

Fox licked and he lapped with his short little snout.
But no matter how hard he tried he could not
get even a mouthful of the meal.

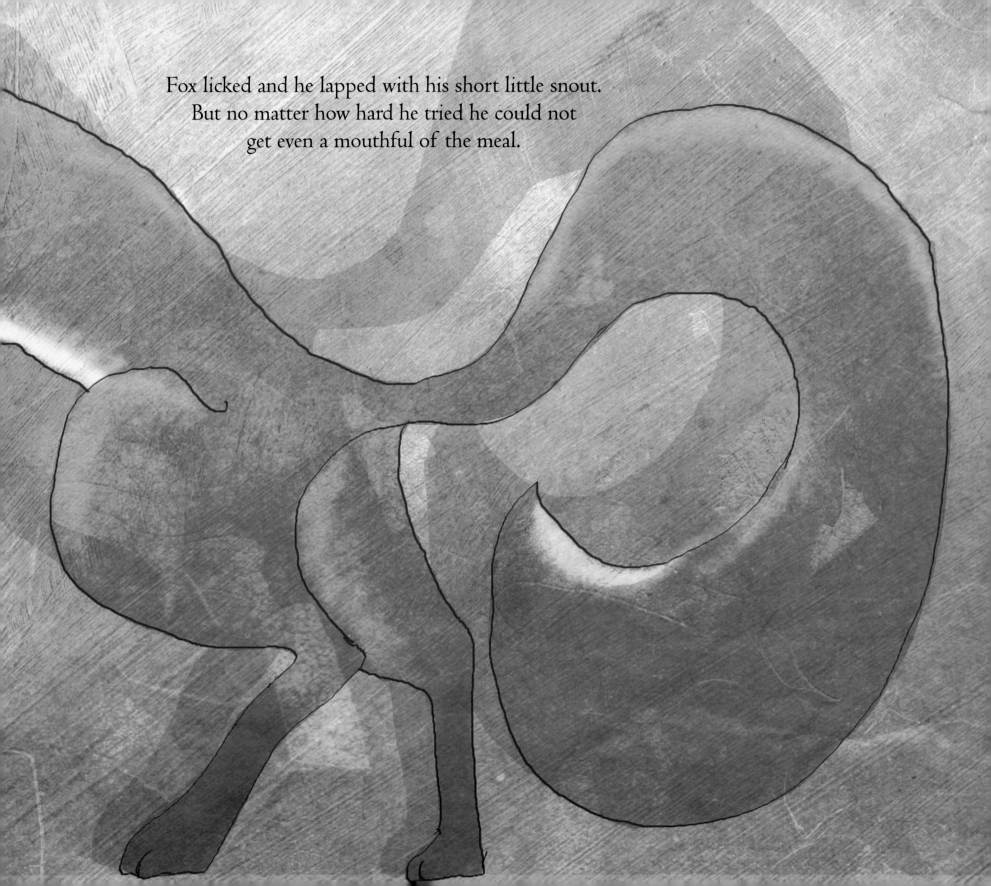

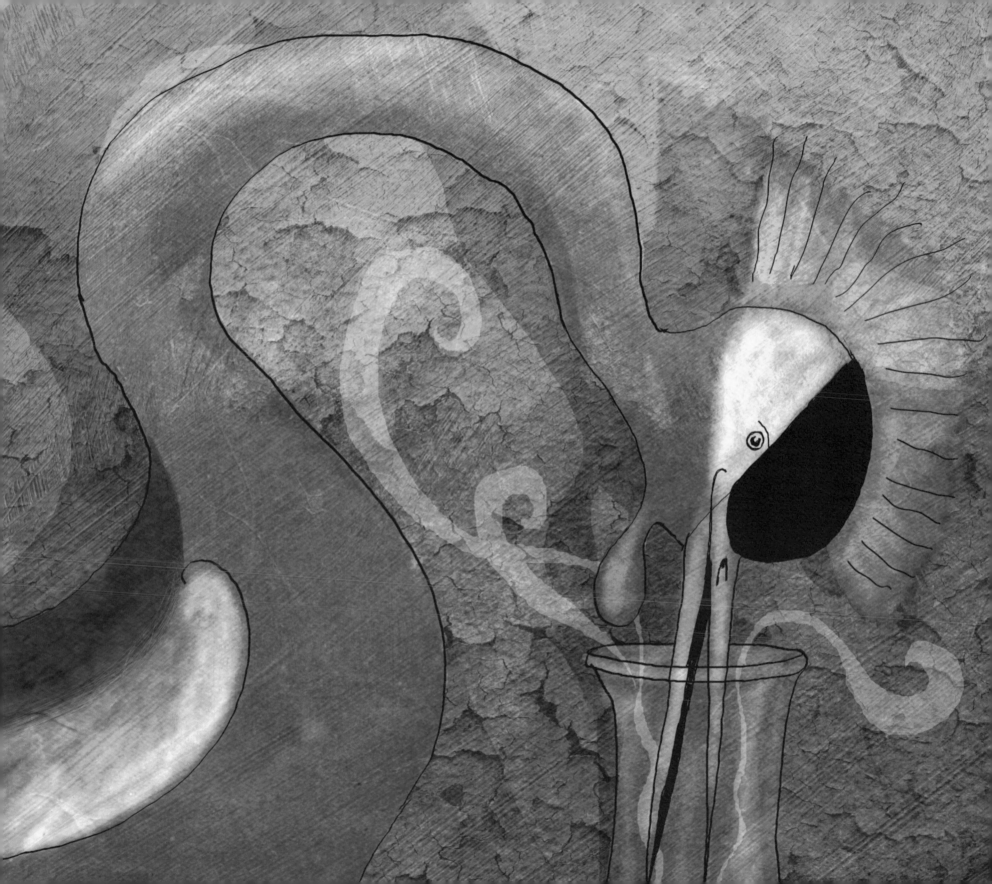

鹤慢慢地吃她的晚餐，细尝每一口的滋味。
「亲爱的狐狸，多谢你到来，」她微笑着说，
「让我能够回敬你的好意。」

狐狸的肚子咯咯隆隆地响，当他回家时，他仍然很饿。

Crane ate her meal very slowly, savouring every mouthful.
"Dear Fox, thank you so much for coming," she smiled,
"it has been a pleasure to repay your kindness."

Fox's tummy gurgled and grumbled.
And when he went home, he was still hungry.

The Fox and the Crane

Writing Activity:
Read the story. Explain that we can write our own fable by changing the characters.

Discuss the different animals you could use, bearing in mind what different kinds of dishes they would need! For example, instead of the fox and the crane you could have a tiny mouse and a tall giraffe.

Write an example together as a class, then give the children the opportunity to write their own. Children who need support could be provided with a writing frame.

Art Activity:
Dishes of every colour and kind! Create them from clay, salt dough, play dough… Make them, paint them, decorate them…

Maths Activity:
Provide a variety of vessels: bowls, jugs, vases, mugs… Children can use these to investigate capacity:

Compare the containers and order them from smallest to largest.

Estimate the capacity of each container.

Young children can use non-standard measures e.g. 'about 3 beakers full'.

Check estimates by filling the container with coloured liquid ('soup') or dry lentils.

Older children can use standard measures such as a litre jug, and measure using litres and millilitres. How near were the estimates?

Label each vessel with its capacity.

The King of the Forest

Writing Activity:
Children can write their own fables by changing the setting of this story. Think about what kinds of animals you would find in a different setting. For example how about 'The King of the Arctic' starring an arctic fox and a polar bear!

Storytelling Activity:
Draw a long path down a roll of paper showing the route Fox took through the forest. The children can add their own details, drawing in the various scenes and re-telling the story orally with model animals.

If you are feeling ambitious you could chalk the path onto the playground so that children can act out the story using appropriate noises and movements! (They could even make masks to wear, decorated with feathers, woollen fur, sequin scales etc.)

Music Activity:
Children choose a forest animal. Then select an instrument that will make a sound that matches the way their animal looks and moves. Encourage children to think about musical features such as volume, pitch and rhythm. For example a loud, low, plodding rhythm played on a drum could represent an elephant.

Children perform their animal sounds. Can the class guess the animal?

Children can play their pieces in groups, to create a forest soundscape.

狐假虎威　－　森林之王

－ 中国语言

The King of the Forest

- a Chinese Fable

retold by Dawn Casey

illustrated by Jago

Mandarin translation
by Sylvia Denham

狐狸正在森林漫步，突然听到草丛中有东西移动。
抖动　　庞大的东西。
眨动　　黄色的眼睛。
闪动　　像利刀的牙齿。

Fox was walking in the forest when he heard something moving
in the long grass.
RUSTLE Something big.
BLINK　 Something with yellow eyes.
FLASH　 Something with teeth like knives.

「早晨，小狐狸，」老虎笑着说，嘴里显露的都是牙齿。

狐狸吞一口气。

「真高兴见到你，」老虎呜呜地说，「我刚刚开始感到肚饿。」

狐狸灵机一触，「你真大胆！」他说，「你难道不知道我是森林之王吗？」

「你？森林之王？」老虎说，跟着便大吼地笑。

「如果你不相信我的话，」狐狸威严地说，「跟在我的后面走，你便会看到所有人都畏惧我。」

「那我便真要看看了，」老虎说。

于是狐狸漫步横越森林，老虎得意地在后面跟随，尾巴提得高高的，直至…

"Good morning little fox," Tiger grinned, and his mouth was nothing but teeth.

Fox gulped.

"I am pleased to meet you," Tiger purred. "I was just beginning to feel hungry."

Fox thought fast. "How dare you!" he said. "Don't you know I'm the King of the Forest?"

"You! King of the Forest?" said Tiger, and he roared with laughter.

"If you don't believe me," replied Fox with dignity, "walk behind me and you'll see – everyone is scared of me."

"This I've got to see," said Tiger.

So Fox strolled through the forest. Tiger followed behind proudly, with his tail held high, until…

嘎嘎！
一只巨大的钩嘴鹰！但那只鹰看了老虎一眼便拍
着翅膀飞进丛林去。
「看到吗？」狐狸说，「所有人都畏惧我呢！」
「简直难以置信！」老虎说。
狐狸继续在森林漫步，老虎轻轻地在后面跟着，
他的尾巴稍微下垂，直至⋯

SQUAWK!
A huge hook-beaked hawk! But the hawk took
one look at Tiger and flapped into the trees.
"See?" said Fox. "Everyone is scared of me!"
"Unbelievable!" said Tiger.
Fox strode on through the forest.
Tiger followed behind lightly,
with his tail drooping slightly,
until. . .

咆吼！

一只大黑熊！但那只黑熊望了老虎一眼便掉进树丛中。

「看到吗？」狐狸说，「所有人都畏惧我呢！」

「简直难以置信！」老虎说。

狐狸继续在森林漫步，老虎卑恭地在后面跟着，

他的尾巴在森林的地上拖着，直至⋯

GROWL!

A big black bear! But the bear took one look
at Tiger and crashed into the bushes.

"See?" said Fox. "Everyone is scared of me!"

"Incredible!" said Tiger.

Fox marched on through the forest. Tiger
followed behind meekly, with his tail
dragging on the forest floor, until…

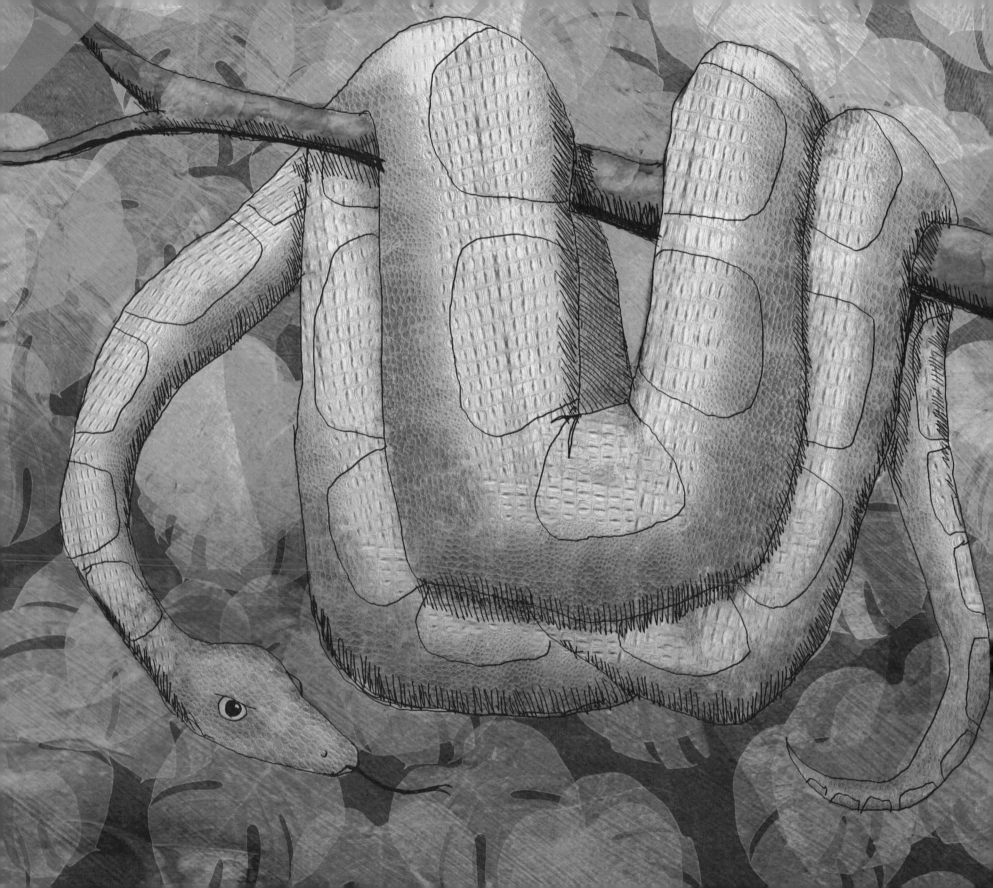

嘶嘶！
一条鬼鬼祟祟溜动着的蛇！但那条蛇望了老虎一眼便滑行到矮树丛去。
「看到吗？」狐狸说，「所有人都畏惧我呢！」

HISSSSSSS!
A slinky slidey snake! But the snake took one look at Tiger and slithered into the undergrowth.
"SEE?" said Fox. "EVERYONE IS SCARED OF ME!"

「我看到了，」老虎说，「你是森林之王，而我是你谦卑的随从。」
「好，」狐狸说，「那么，你便走吧！」

于是老虎便夹着尾巴畏缩地走了。

"I do see," said Tiger, "you are the King of the Forest and I am your humble servant."
"Good," said Fox. "Then, be gone!"

And Tiger went, with his tail between his legs.

「森林之王，」狐狸对自己笑着说，他的微笑变成咧嘴露齿的笑，咧嘴露齿的笑变成吃吃地笑，狐狸大声地笑着回家。

"King of the Forest," said Fox to himself with a smile. His smile grew into a grin, and his grin grew into a giggle, and Fox laughed out loud all the way home.

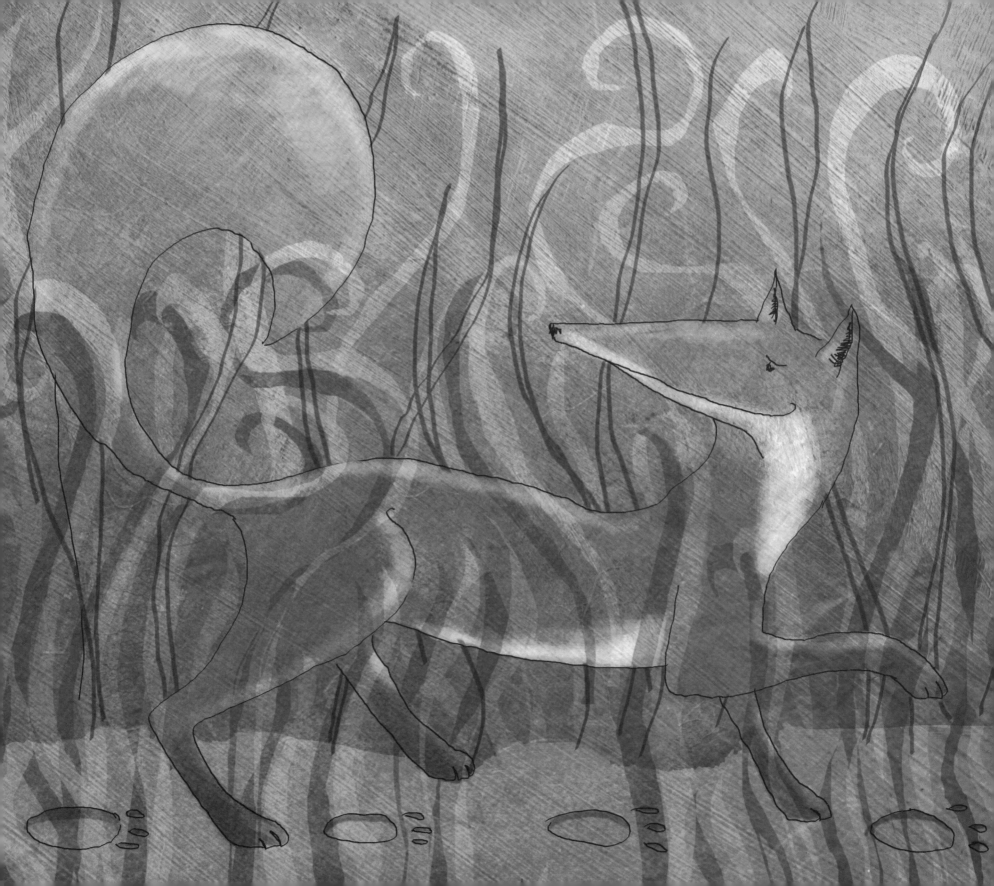

To my Nana, with love - DC
For my wife, Alex - J

First published in 2006 by Mantra Lingua Ltd
Global House, 303 Ballards Lane
London N12 8NP
www.mantralingua.com

Printed in Norwich, UK. 2M100317PB04170047

A CIP record for this book is available from the British Library